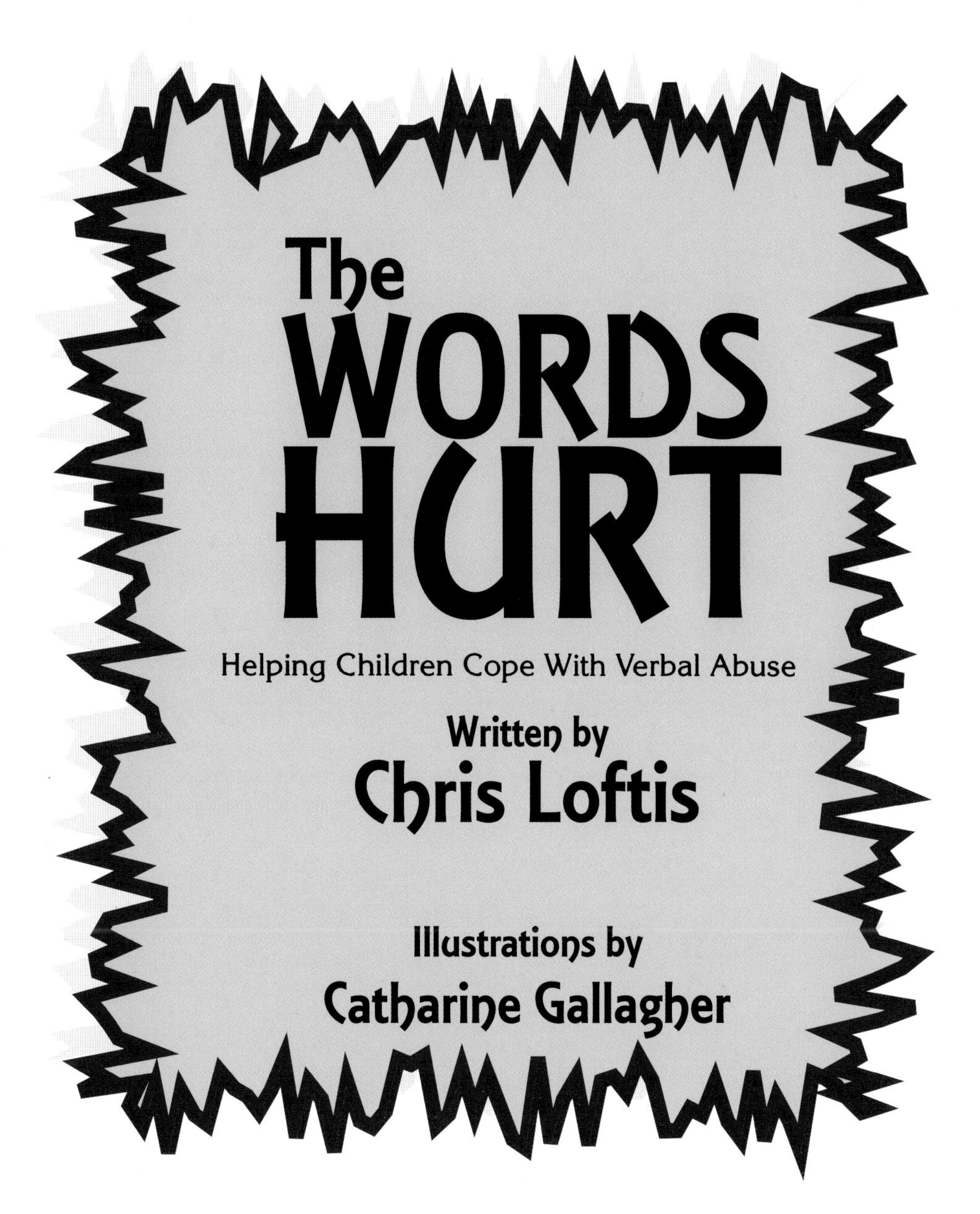

The WORDS HURT

Helping Children Cope With Verbal Abuse

Written by
Chris Loftis

Illustrations by
Catharine Gallagher

Library of Congress Catalog Card Number: 94-66754

Loftis, Chris
The Words Hurt

ISBN 10: 0-88282-132-6
ISBN 13: 978-0-88282-132-0

SMALL HORIZONS
A Division of New Horizon Press

Visit us on the web at: newhorizonpressbooks.com

2010 2009 2008 2007 2006 / 6 5 4 3 2

Printed in Hong Kong

Author's note: My professional background includes working in a group home that served children experiencing serious difficulties with their parents, their teachers, or with the authorities... usually all three. I was often asked to go to children's homes for interviews with parents and other family members. While I found many to be earnest and hard working people, I also saw many who used shame as a sort of a weapon to control their kids.

I remember being ashamed of myself a few times when I was little. Still, it wasn't because my parents were pushing me to feel that way so I would do what they wanted me to do. I was lucky. My parents were firm but fair, and their words were almost always encouraging.

This is a story about words. Words can hurt and words can heal. They have power and they have impact. Sometimes people are very careless with them. They use them like fishing lines... trying to reel them back in if they don't bring in the right catch. But words aren't like that. Once they are out in the air, they have a tendency to stay for a while, especially words spoken in anger or shouted in threat.

I hope the words chosen to tell the story will give you a good place...to begin or continue your lifelong dialogue of love - called family.

The words hurt.
They hurt badly,
and they stayed in the air
for a long
long
time.

Greg listened
and tried to believe he meant something else;
in his head, he repeated them
line by line.

But no matter how the words
were replayed in his head,
they stayed there
cruel and mean.
And his hurt didn't change or go away
even after his dad apologized and said
he was "just blowin' off a little steam."

Greg's dad never ever hit him,
even when Greg would do things
that would make his dad so very mad!
But Boy,
could he yell !
When he yelled at you,
it was the worst
chewing out you've ever had !

He seemed to know just what to say,
just what would hurt the most.
Sometimes,
he would come back and apologize,
but as Mom always says:
"You can't make dinner rolls
out of burnt toast."

No... once words are out there,
you can't just reel them back in.
You can't make them go away
with just a wink
or a wish
or a grin.

At night,
Greg would sit in his bed
and wonder
if what his dad said was true.
He'd wonder
if his dad really meant what he said,
and he'd wonder
how much his dad really knew.

And do you know what?
As nice a kid as Greg was,
and as hard as he tried to do the right thing,
the words his father yelled at him
would sit there in his head,
and in his heart
be a terrible,
terrible
thing.

You see,
there was always a little bit of truth
in what his dad was saying,
enough to leave some doubt...
as to
was he right
or
was he wrong;
was he in
or was he out?

He'd wonder
if other kids' dads yelled so loudly
whenever they were late for school.
He'd wonder if all dads got this mad at their kids.
He'd wonder if cleaning your room
was every home's
VERY SERIOUS rule.

Greg also wondered why,
after dad started yelling,
his mom would always just leave the house,
and why,
at dinner time,
no one would say anything...
each of them...
just as quiet as a mouse.

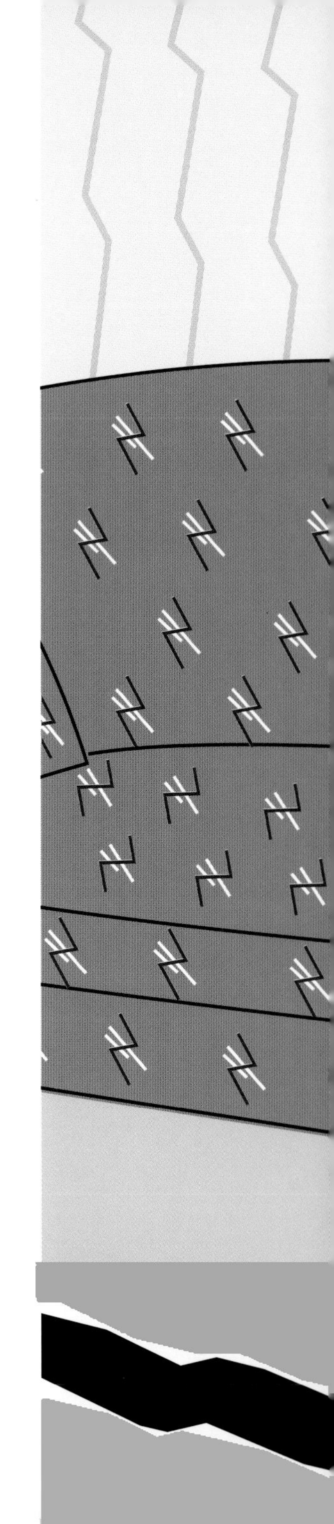

Greg figured whatever it was,
his dad was his dad
and so he must be right.
He must not be a good enough son.
That was the conclusion he'd
come to...
alone...
in his bed...
at night...

One day
at the ball park,
Greg was playing with some friends.
When his dad came by to pick him up,
he yelled
"GREG, IT'S TIME TO COME IN."

But Greg was talking
to his best friend in the whole wide world,
a friendly fellow named Joe.
He really didn't hear his dad call,
so he had no way to know

that his dad
was walking up behind them
with a look that meant he was REALLY mad!
He got up to Greg and Joe
and then he
REALLY YELLED
at the little lad.

Greg's dad told him,
in no uncertain terms,
that he was the worst son
that there could EVER BE.
He said he wished that just once
Greg would do as he was told
and offer his dad
something other than
MIS-ER-Y !

Greg's dad went on
and on
while Greg looked down,
wishing he could disappear.
Poor Joe
just stood there with his pal...
embarrassed
for everyone there.

Joe's parents walked up on the scene
and thought it best to interrupt.
Joe's mom said. "Hi, Gang!
How's it going, Joe?
Did you catch any pop ups?"

"Sure did, Mom.
I caught seven
and Greg here made a bunch of good catches!"
"Well, THAT'S GREAT, GREG!
Maybe we can sit with your parents
at some of your matches."

"MOMMM," Joe moaned.
"Matches are in tennis; baseball has games,"
he said with a laugh.
"Well, whatever,"
Joe"s dad said, holding his nose,
"Come along, Baby Ruth;
it's time you had a bath!"

Joe's dad put Joe up on his shoulders.
His mom nodded and turned away,
leaving Greg with his dad
standing there looking down
at the ground
while all around
children laughed and played.

Greg looked up
at his Dad's red face
and then he glanced at Joe's family
walking
through the dimming light.
And Greg felt
guilty somehow
for wishing
that he could go
to THAT home tonight..

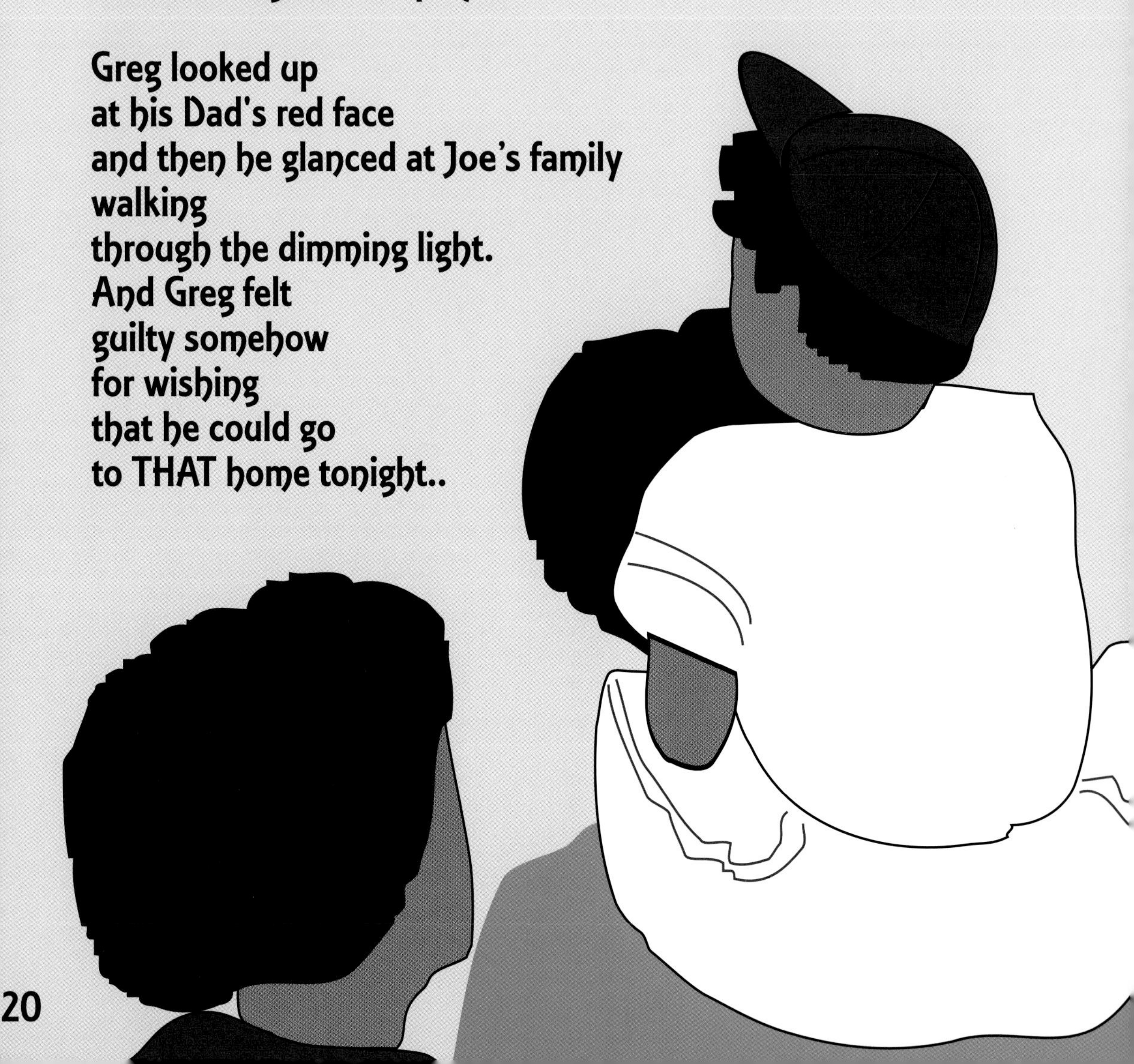

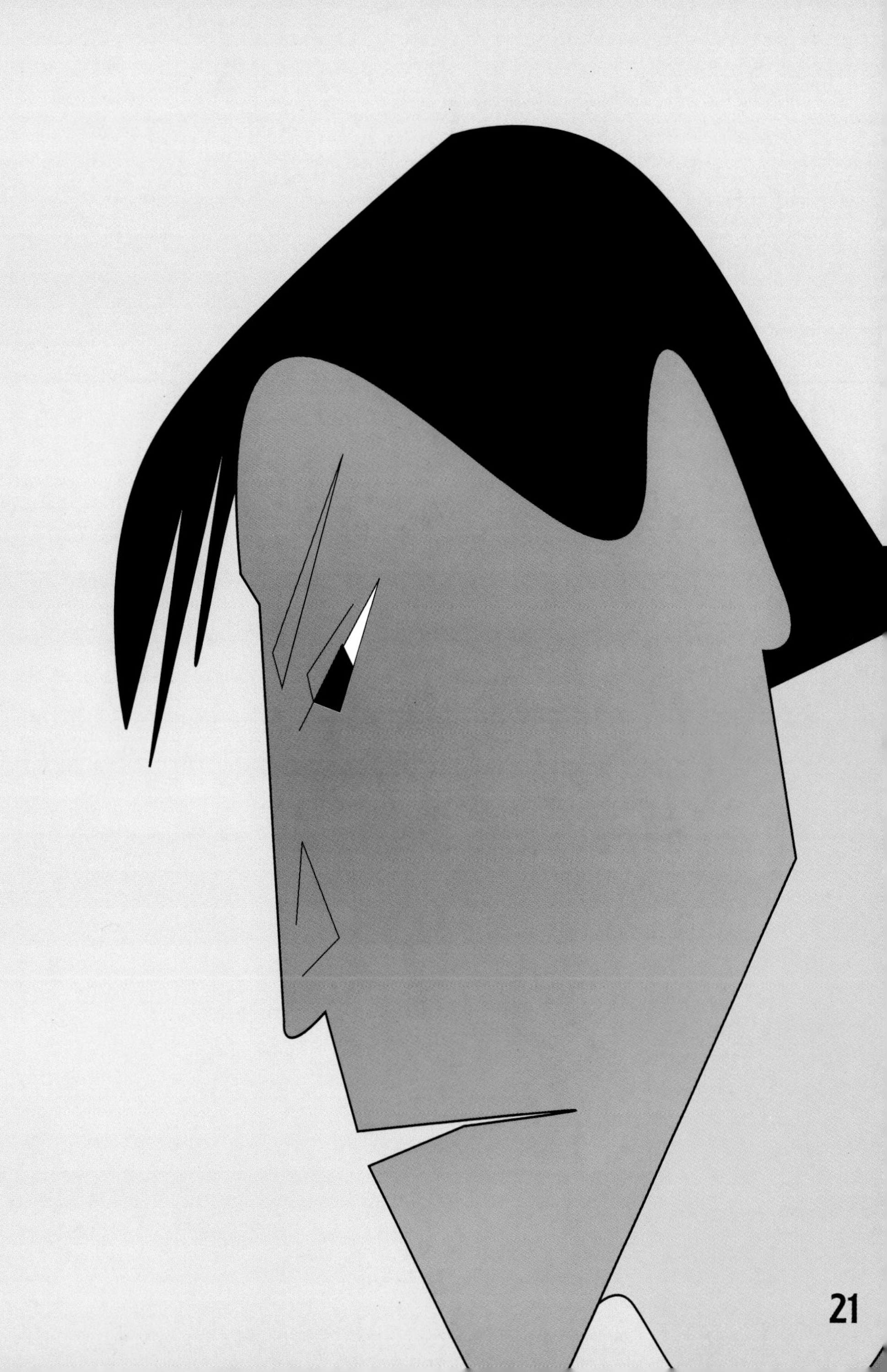

Well,
as they always do,
the next day came
and it was a perfect time to play ball.
So, after school,
Greg met with Joe
and they raced up the street
past the mall.

Then,
down the alley
and up the hill they ran
until they reached the edge of the bases.
And as they walked across the green grass,
they could see their fathers in the stands
with what looked like VERY angry faces.

The two boys
couldn't make out what the two men
were saying
but there was obvious tension.
Greg turned to Joe
and said,
"I'm sorry, man
but my dad gets angry real easy."
Joe said,
"Well, I was going to mention..."

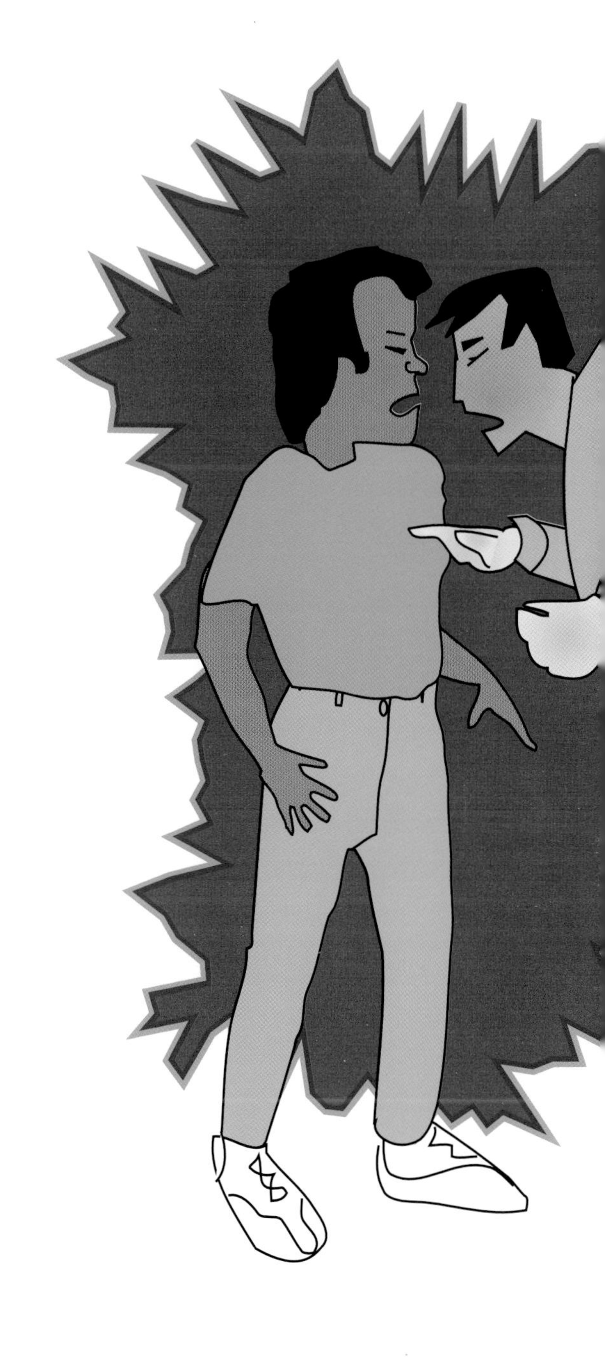

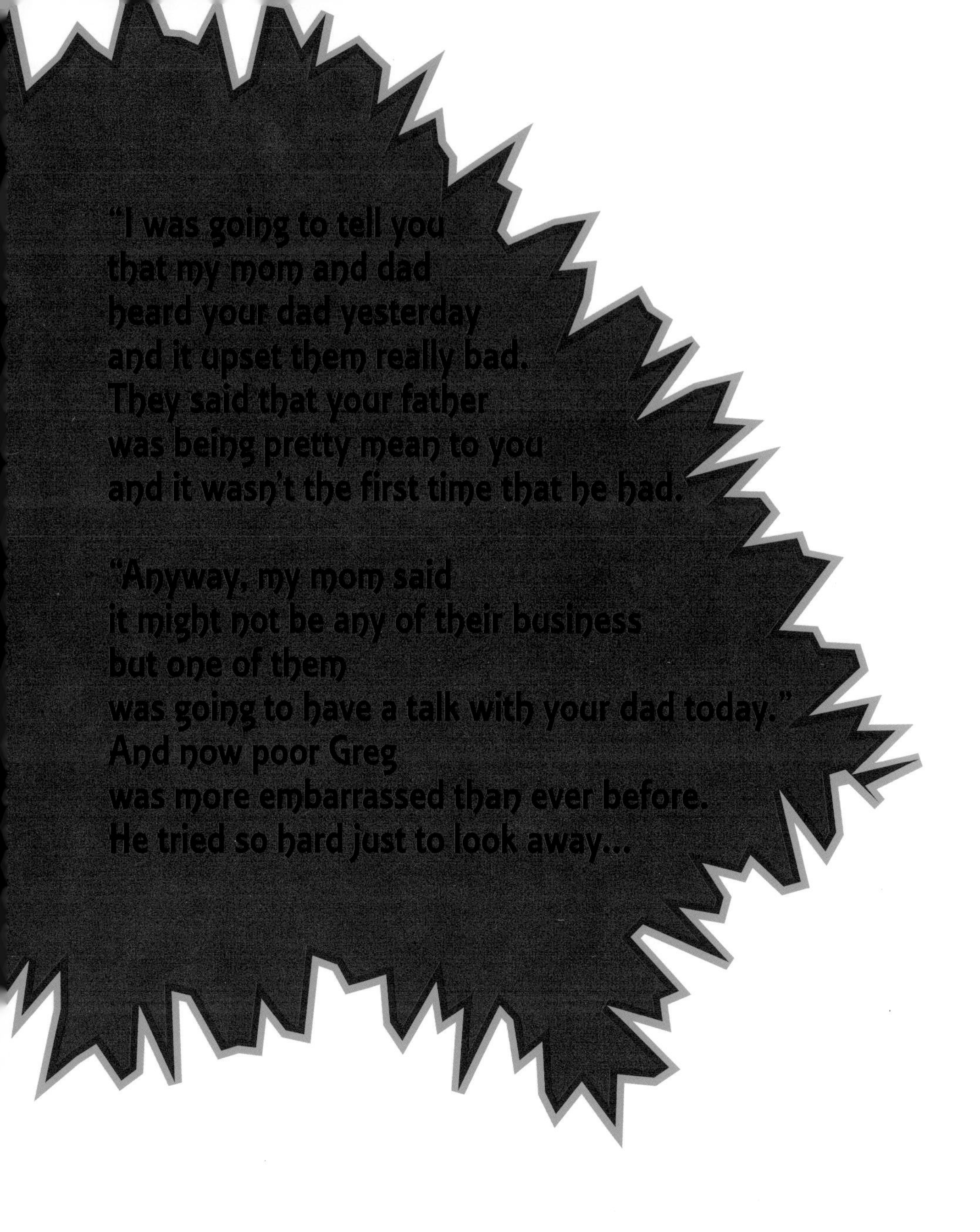

"I was going to tell you
that my mom and dad
heard your dad yesterday
and it upset them really bad.
They said that your father
was being pretty mean to you
and it wasn't the first time that he had.

"Anyway, my mom said
it might not be any of their business
but one of them
was going to have a talk with your dad today."
And now poor Greg
was more embarrassed than ever before.
He tried so hard just to look away...

But he couldn't...

he wanted to hear
every
single
word.

He wanted
Joe's dad to give it to him
and to give it to him
good!

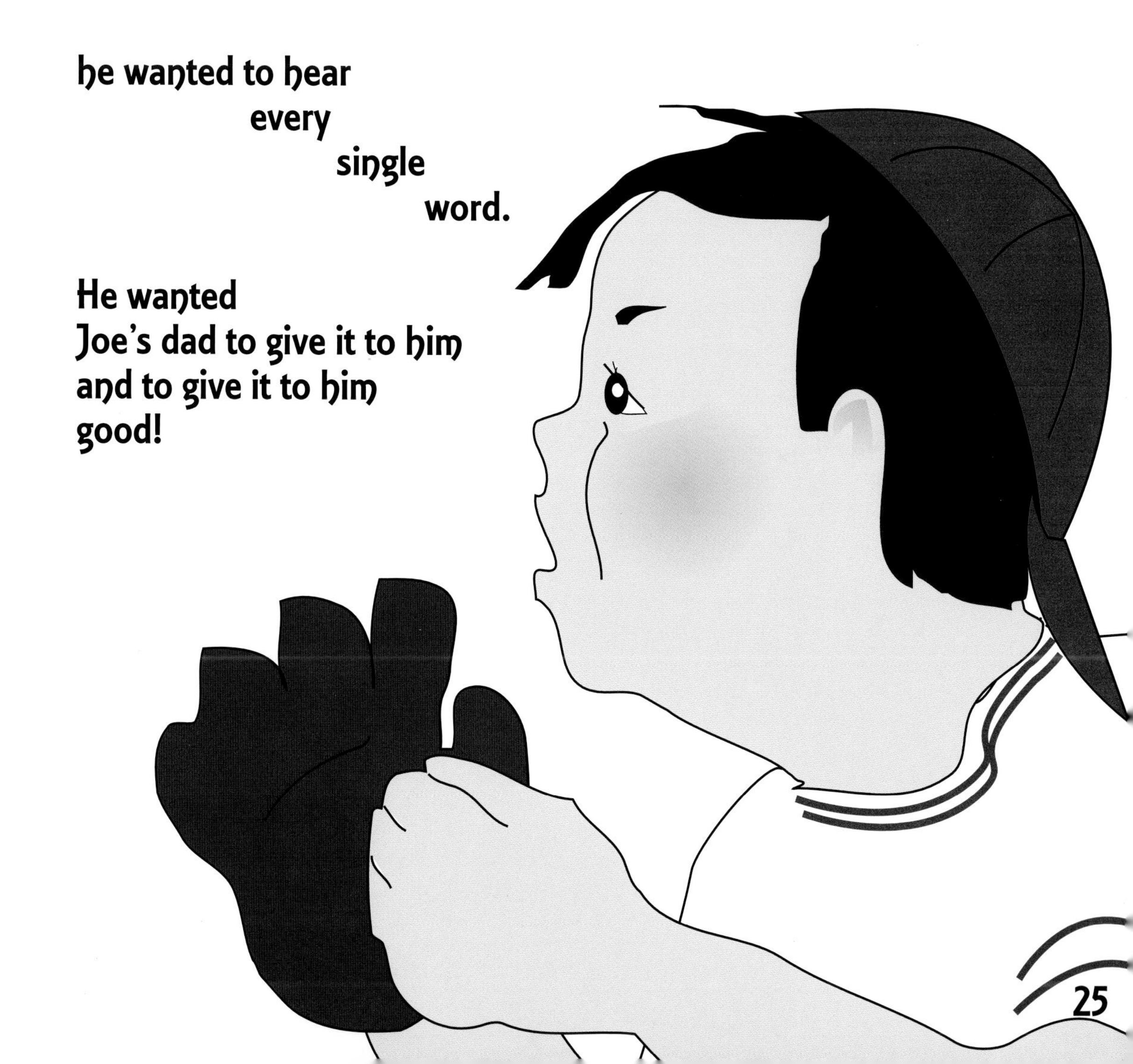

After a few minutes passed,
Greg's dad yelled,
"GREG,
GET IN THAT CAR!"
and they drove away.
They hadn't gone very far

when Greg's dad blurted,
"THE NERVE OF THAT MAN...
telling me that I abuse my child.
Why,
I'd like to see him work two jobs
or in my shoes
walk a mile.

"Why,
your mom and I work on the house,
not to mention
the FULL TIME job
of keeping this family whole!
To suggest
that I AM HARMING my child,
well, I just don't-even-know..."

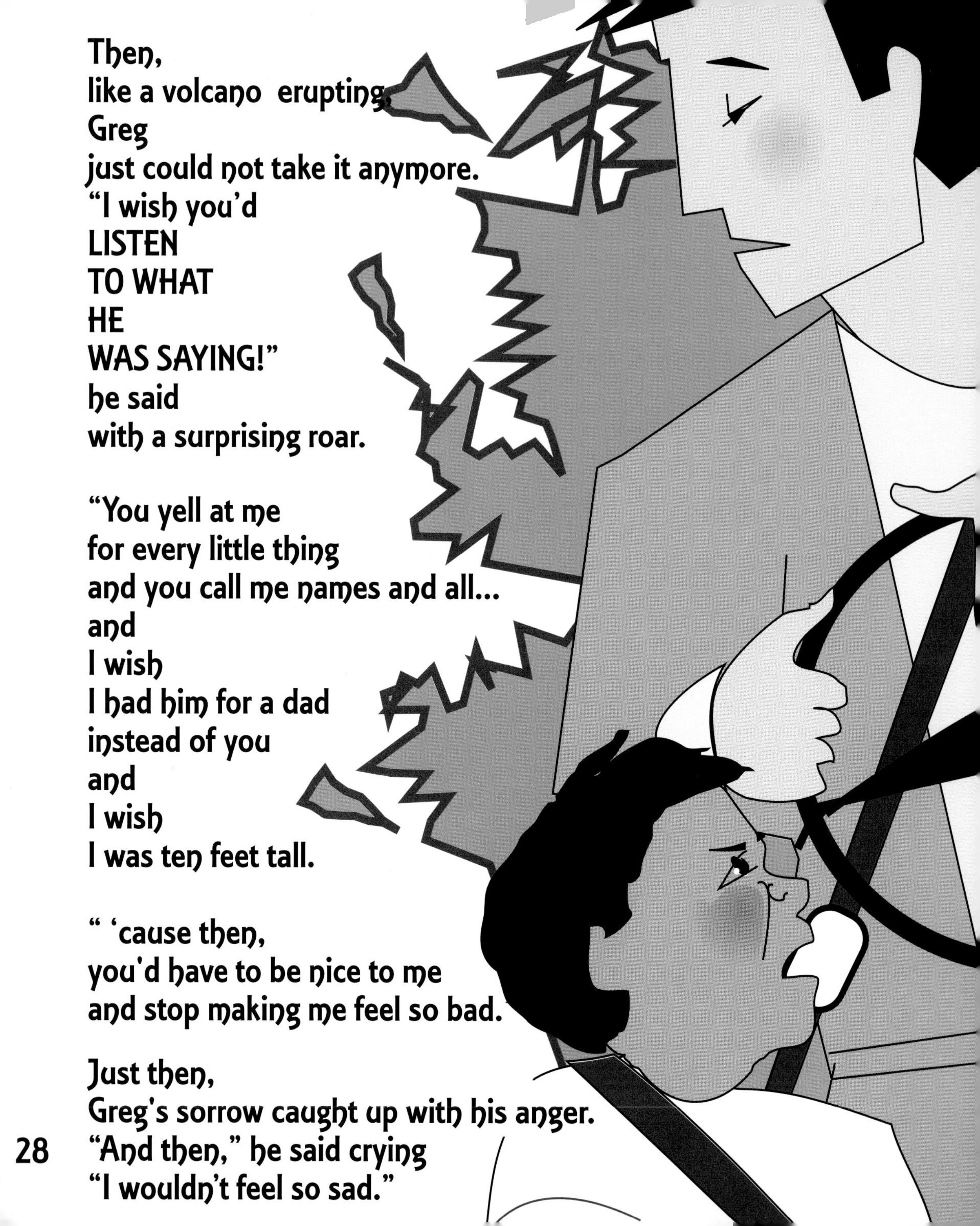

Then,
like a volcano erupting,
Greg
just could not take it anymore.
"I wish you'd
LISTEN
TO WHAT
HE
WAS SAYING!"
he said
with a surprising roar.

"You yell at me
for every little thing
and you call me names and all...
and
I wish
I had him for a dad
instead of you
and
I wish
I was ten feet tall.

" 'cause then,
you'd have to be nice to me
and stop making me feel so bad.

Just then,
Greg's sorrow caught up with his anger.
"And then," he said crying
"I wouldn't feel so sad."

Greg's dad stopped the car
right where they were
and he looked into his son's red and swollen eyes.
Then, in a sweet...
almost trembling voice
the man said,
"Oh son,
how I wish you were telling me lies.

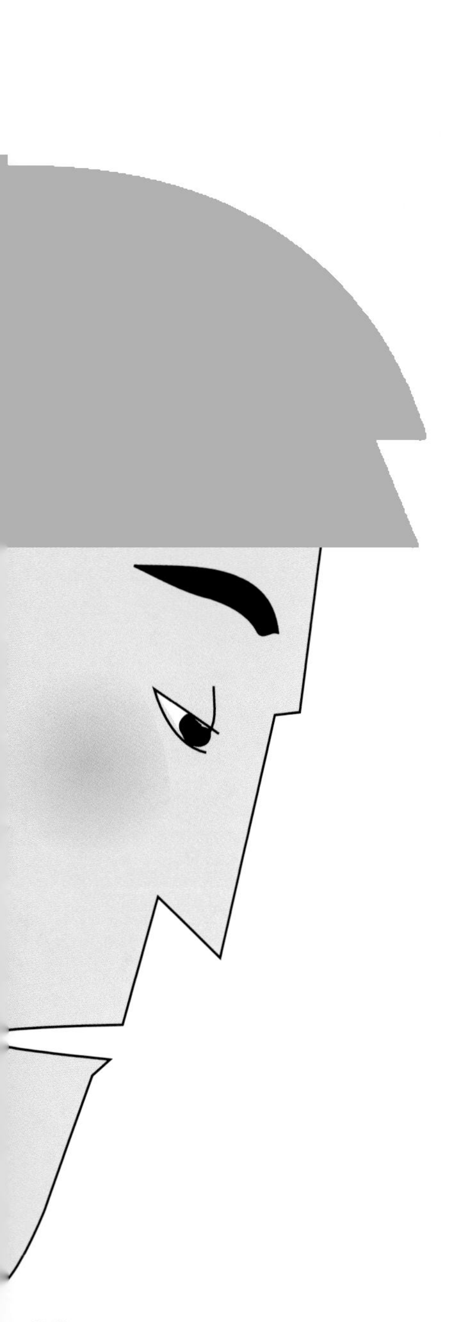

"I wish
I'd never yelled at you once.
And I wish
that I could always make you smile.
I wish
I was one of those guys
who always said the right thing.
Shoooh... maybe even
every once in a while.

"I wish
I wasn't so tired at the end of the day
and I wish
I didn't feel so old.
Boy, I tell you,
when I look
in the mirror,
I see an old man,
one that sometimes,
even I don't know."

With that,
Greg reached over
and wiped a tear away
from his father's own reddened eyes.
He put his little arms
around his dad's giant shoulders
and said,
"It's okay, Daddy,
you don't need to cry.

"And I love you, Dad.
I'm going to do better;
I'll make you proud;
you'll see."

His father reached over,
put his finger to the boy's lips
and said
"Shhhhh...
We both know
it's me."

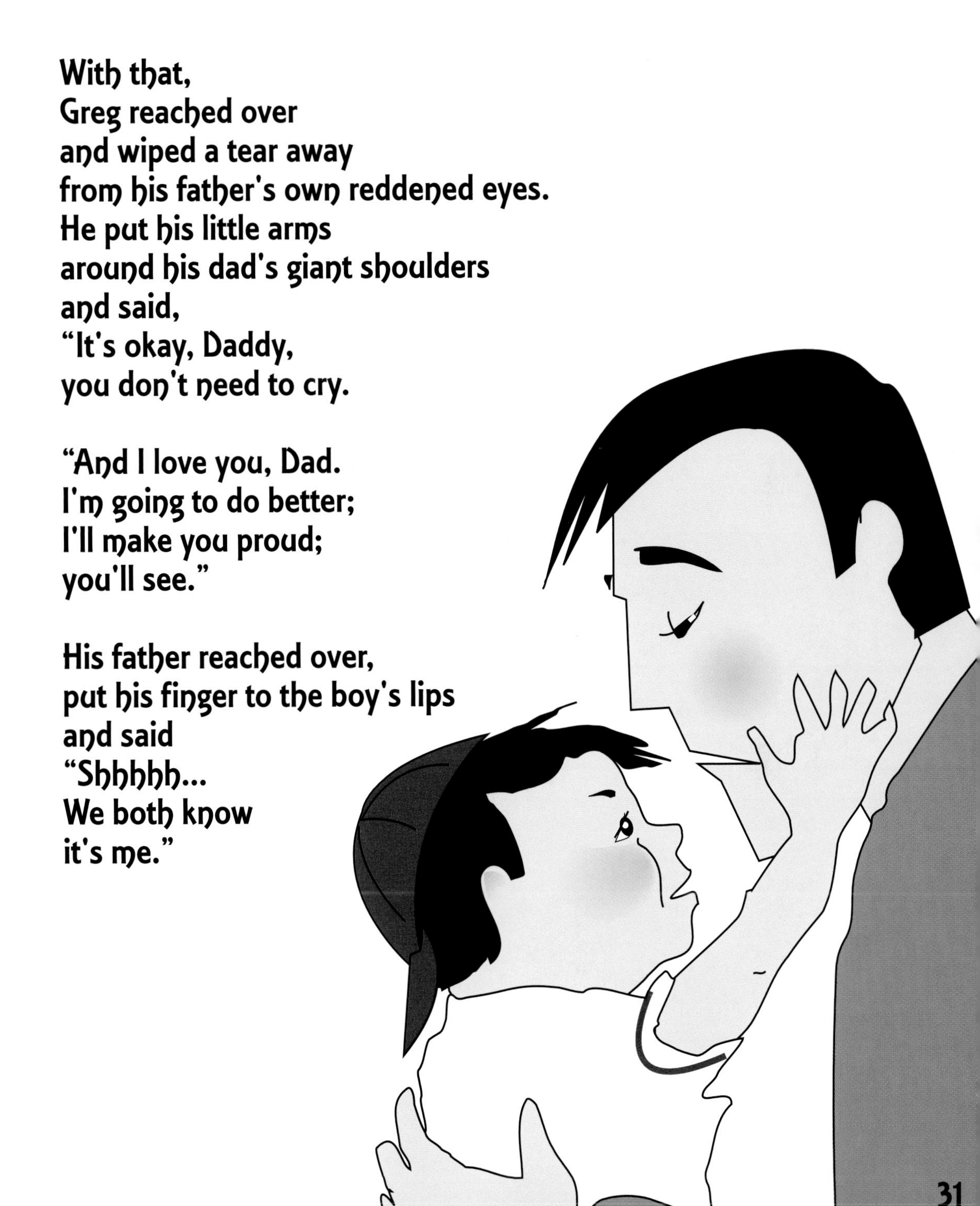

"WHAT'S THE PROBLEM?"
The officer asked.
"Why have you stopped here
in the middle of the road?"

"No problem."
Greg and his father said
at the same time.
They both laughed.
Greg said,
"Come on, Dad.
Let's go."

And go they did,
home to Mom
where they all had a very long talk.
They decided
they needed to get some real help
with all of this
and they decided to take a walk.

You know,
a walk can take you to forever
or
it can take you down the street.
But,
to get where you need to go to,
you have to decide
to start moving your feet.

You have to decide
there is a place
that is worth the effort
and a place that is worth the time.
Like Greg and his dad in the car that day,
sometimes,
sorrow
helps you
your courage find.

No one said anything.
They all just walked along.
They were all thinking of different things,
their hearts
all singing different songs.

Mom
was thinking
this was just the thing this family needed
to help get them through their troubles.
So many times,
she had heard her husband's anger
but she didn't want to burst his bubble.

She knew
he was under a lot of pressure
and she wanted everything to be good.
Now,
she realized,
that you can't just
wish things to work out right
even though we all wish we could.

You
have to address your troubles.
You
have to take them straight on.
If you don't,
they just get worse and worse,
my friends
and the bad days
become longer than long.

Dad
was going over all the things he'd said to Greg.
He knew
he must learn to deal with his anger.
He couldn't
just keep throwing it at his family,
or pretty soon
they would all be strangers.

Anger is a powerful thing,
and a child
is usually not.
Sometimes adults
figure kids won't really remember.
Greg seemed to remember
a lot.

Greg's father
did not want to be remembered
the way that he sadly
remembered his own Dad.
His father could sometimes be very cruel
and he didn't like
the memories he had.

The idea
that he was doing the same thing
was something
for which there was simply no excuse.
There's no reason
in this whole wide world
to harm a little child,
be it your hands
or your words
that do the abuse.

And he was going to do it.
He was going to get the help
for which he was in need.
And he was bound and determined
that this kind of anger
would never again in his family's field
take seed.

Greg
was thinking
about what his dad had said in the car,
just before they had to go.
He really does have a lot on his mind
and Greg really does
love him so.

Greg thought
of how they used to play in the back yard,
back when he was just a kid.
He thought
about how his dad never found him
when they played hide-and-go-seek,
even though Greg
never really did a very good job
when he hid.

And
he thought
of all the good days,

when everything was right...

when Dad's face offered sunshine
and his words offered light.

He thought
about what Joe's dad had said
about his dad's yelling being abuse.
Greg had always thought
that meant beating up a kid,
until their body was all black and blue.

But
when you think about it,
not all blows are made by the hand
and not all whipping is done with a belt.
Greg thought about some of the things
his dad had said to him
and how beaten up he'd felt.

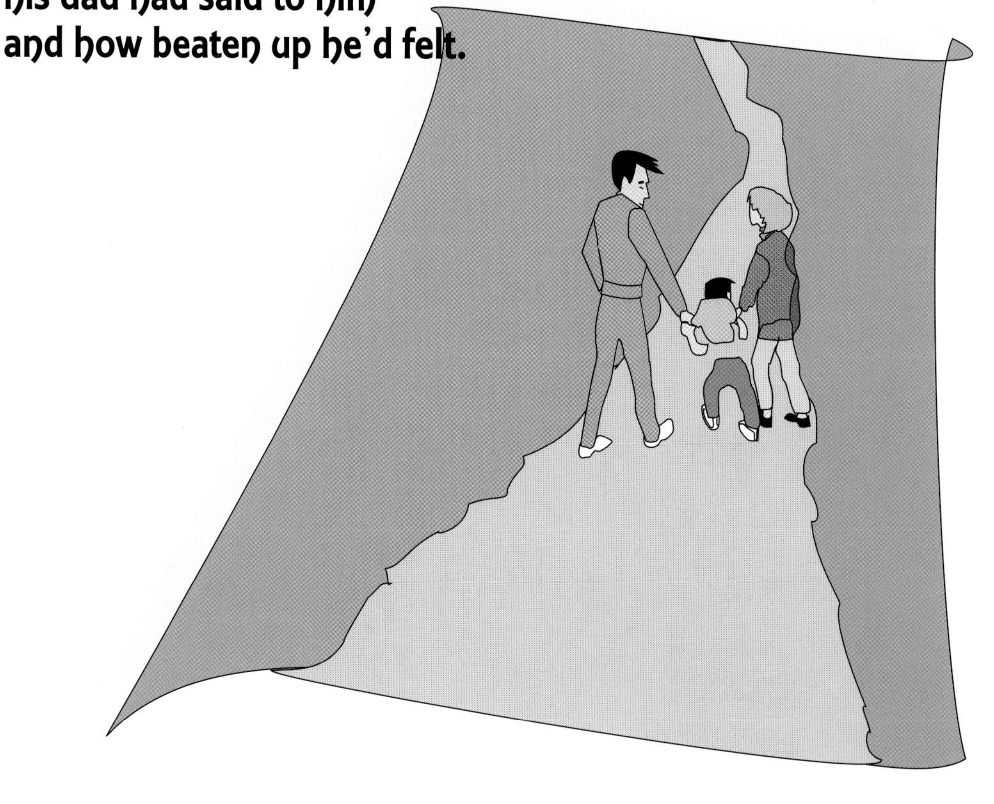

As
the family
walked around the block for the third time,
Greg's parents looked at him
and squeezed his tiny hands.
His father knelt down,
kissed Greg's forehead,
and whispered,
"I'm so proud of you
my little man."

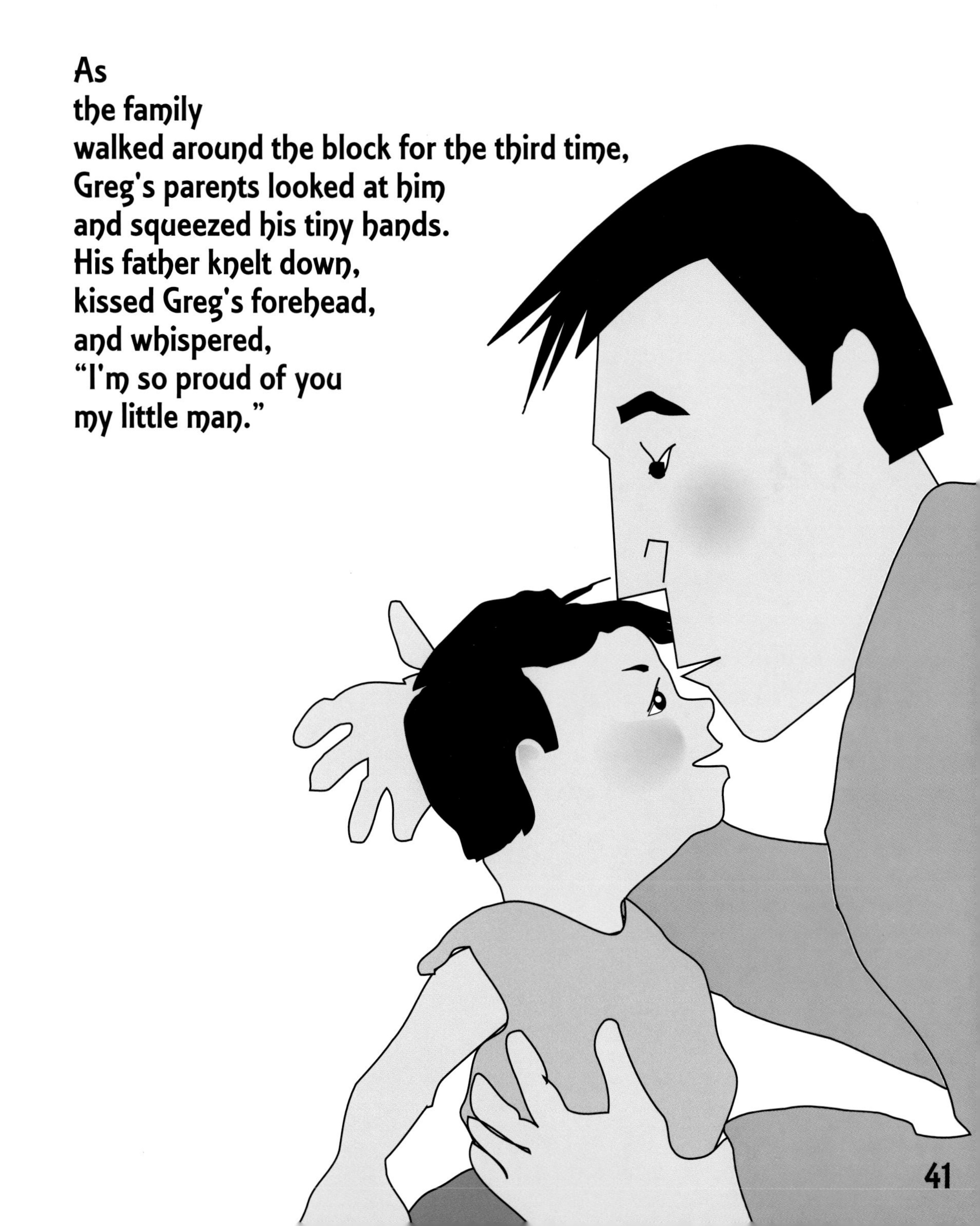

And do you know what?
If painful words can last forever,
kind ones
can last
just as long.
Greg felt like he'd been touched by an angel,
like he'd heard the world's
prettiest song.

And if Dad's yelling
had broken into his heart
and his spirit begun to steal,
that soft look
    and those kind words
had his heart
    and his family
begun
to heal.

Thank you
for sharing
this story
with me...
Chris

Tips for Parent and Educators

(1) Use positive words when criticizing: negative words such as stupid, worst, ugly or dumb can leave a lasting impression on children, often influencing their self perception.

(2) Children remember more than you might think: you may forget what you said last week but a child doesn't, your words will last in his or her mind.

(3) Don't blame a child for your own mistakes or problems: make sure you aren't venting your own frustrations on the child.

(4) Don't place the responsibility of your emotions on the child, blaming him or her for your feelings puts unneeded guilt on the child.

(5) Verbal abuse can happen at any volume, but screaming or yelling can frighten a child. Not only will the abuse hurt the child psychologically, but the fright will influence how he or she views you.

(6) It does not take a loud outburst to verbally abuse a child, even when avoiding yelling a child can sustain great emotional hurt through intimidating looks, words or gestures.

(7) When a loved one verbally abuses a child do not tell him or her to "ignore it" or explain "that's just the way that person is". One technique is to confront the abuser about his or her behavior. This will show the child abuse is wrong and also let the child know he or she is valued.

(8) Let children communicate choice; this will allow children greater responsibility and give them the ability to stand up for themselves.

(9) Never humiliate a child in public, it sabotages self esteem.

(10) Always try to correct a child's mistakes or misbehaviors in private.

(11) Take children's concerns seriously. Don't minimize them.

(12) Make children feel safe.

(13) Start a constructive dialogue between yourself and the child rather than interrogating or accusing the child.

(14) Seek professional help for a child who feels demeaned and shaken and whose self-confidence has been compromised.

Tips for Kids

(1) If you are being bullied or teased and feel unsafe call or find an adult you trust.

(2) When an adult is abusive to you, it is all right to tell that person how you feel. Be sure to do this in a safe environment. Sometimes adults forget how much words can hurt.

(3) If you feel too afraid to confront the abusive person, tell an adult such as a teacher or parent.

(4) Remember, just as others' words can hurt you, your words can hurt others. Kids sometimes gang up on others and tease them; don't join in on the teasing, tell a parent or teacher about the situation.

(5) Take care of yourself. Don't abuse yourself or others. Accept that you are a good person and deserve to be treated kindly.

(6) It's not your fault when people verbally attack you. Try not to take their words to heart.

(7) Remember how it feels to be picked on or teased. Treat others the way you would want to be treated.

(8) Choose a code word to use with family or friends so they will know when you need help.

(9) Trust your feelings. Fear, nightmares and anger can be warning signs that something is wrong with the way you are being treated by adults in your life. Tell someone you trust you need help.

(10) Don't be ashamed to visit a counselor if you feel extremely angry or hurt, because someone is mistreating you. You can express your deepest feelings to these professionals and feel safe. Talking to them will help you feel better.